When God Made
Santa Claus

Mr. Greg

Illustrated by
Ann Rymsza

God gave his only son to be born.
Into a world shattered and torn.

On that day the angels did sing.
Crown Him Lord above, King of Kings.
Into the world came goodness and light.
On that sacred and most holy night.

Later, God watched the world become unstable. "I must remind them of that night in the stable."

In the midst of wars and our collective flaws
That's when God created Santa Claus.

God filled him with the gift of Christmas Spirit.
Gave him a laugh so big all could hear it.

Gave him the gift of Christmas Joy,
Shared with a child a brand new toy.

Gave him the power to see every child everywhere,

Anytime, any place, anywhere.

This was a time for kids to be good,
And a time for the adults to do as they should.
Yes, there was great cheer and applause
When God made Santa Claus.

Santa will tell you the spirit of the season
"Let Emmanuel's birth be the foremost reason."

Wherever we see the Christmas lights,
Let's remember the light of Christ.
When we see the sturdy Christmas tree,
Be mindful of His love that saved you and me.

With these gifts that we exchange
It's only God's love that can bring change.

He cleansed our sins with his death and tears.
His birth will be remembered for years and years.

Know that God doesn't do anything just because,
God knew what He was doing when he made Santa Claus.

The End

About the Author

Mr. Greg has made a positive difference in the lives of young people, for over 30 years, through his work in schools, camps, and coaching. Mr. Greg has been writing stories, poems, and song lyrics since he was a young man. It was only after he became the father of four fabulous kids, that his creative focus turned towards children's stories.

WestBow Press books may be ordered through booksellers or by contacting:

WestBow Press
A Division of Thomas Nelson & Zondervan
1663 Liberty Drive
Bloomington, IN 47403
www.westbowpress.com
1 (866) 928-1240

Because of the dynamic nature of the Internet, any web addresses or links contained in this book may have changed since publication and may no longer be valid. The views expressed in this work are solely those of the author and do not necessarily reflect the views of the publisher, and the publisher hereby disclaims any responsibility for them.

ISBN: 978-1-5127-5196-3 (sc)
ISBN: 978-1-5127-5197-0 (e)

Library of Congress Control Number: 2016912540

Print information available on the last page.

WestBow Press rev. date: 08/29/2016

WESTBOW
PRESS®
A DIVISION OF THOMAS NELSON
& ZONDERVAN

CPSIA information can be obtained
at www.ICGtesting.com
Printed in the USA
LVOW05s2131121016
508359LV00004B/4/P